HARLEY QUINN'S
MaDCaP CaPeRs

The Harley and Batgirl Show

by Michael Anthony Steele
illustrated by Sarah Leuver

Batman created by Bob Kane with Bill Finger

STONE ARCH BOOKS
a capstone imprint

Published by Stone Arch Books, an imprint of Capstone.
1710 Roe Crest Drive
North Mankato, Minnesota 56003
capstonepub.com

Library of Congress Cataloging-in-Publication Data
Names: Steele, Michael Anthony, author. | Leuver, Sarah, illustrator. |
   Kane, Bob, creator. | Finger, Bill, 1914–1974, creator.
Title: The Harley and Batgirl show / by Michael Anthony Steele ;
   illustrated by Sarah Leuver.
Description: North Mankato, Minnesota : Stone Arch Books, an imprint
   of Capstone [2022] | Series: Harley Quinn's madcap capers | "Batman
   created by Bob Kane with Bill Finger." | Audience: Ages 8–11. |
   Audience: Grades 4–6. | Summary: Harley has her own reality TV
   show with a film crew following her around taping her doing fake
   robberies, and Batgirl finds herself as a suspicious and unwilling
   co-star—but when the film crew turns out to be a pack of thieves using
   Harley, the angry burglar teams up with the skeptical crime fighter to
   catch the villains.
Identifiers: LCCN 2021030711 (print) | LCCN 2021030712 (ebook) |
   ISBN 9781663975379 (hardcover) | ISBN 9781666329773 (paperback) |
   ISBN 9781666329780 (pdf)
Subjects: LCSH: Harley Quinn (Fictitious character)—Juvenile fiction. |
   Batgirl (Fictitious character)—Juvenile fiction. | Supervillains--Juvenile
   fiction. | Superheroes—Juvenile fiction. | Reality television
   programs—Juvenile fiction. | Theft—Juvenile fiction. | CYAC:
   Supervillains—Fiction. | Superheroes—Fiction. | Reality television
   programs—Fiction. | Stealing—Fiction. | LCGFT: Superhero fiction.
Classification: LCC PZ7.S8147 Har 2022 (print) | LCC PZ7.S8147 (ebook)
   | DDC 813.6 [Fic]—dc23
LC record available at https://lccn.loc.gov/2021030711
LC ebook record available at https://lccn.loc.gov/2021030712

Designed by Kay Fraser

Printed and bound in the USA.   4608

TABLE OF CONTENTS

HARLEY QUINN's

MaDCaP CaPeRs

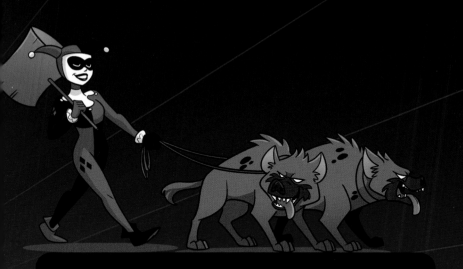

Dr. Harleen Quinzel was once a successful psychiatrist at Gotham City's Arkham Asylum. But everything changed when she met the Joker. As the Clown Prince of Crime shared his heartbreaking—yet fake—story of a troubled childhood, Harleen's heart melted. She soon helped the Joker escape and joined him as a jolly jester with a calling for crime. Now she clowns around Gotham City, and these are . . .

HARLEY QUINN'S MADCAP CAPERS!

CHAPTER 1

Opening Credits

"Ooh! How about that one?!" Harley Quinn asked as she pointed to the large diamond necklace in the display case.

The nervous jewelry store clerk fumbled with his key ring. "Let me just find the correct key . . ."

Harley raised her oversized mallet over her head. "Don't worry. My key opens everything!"

The clerk ducked as Harley smashed the glass case.

KRASH! Bits of broken glass fell away as she pulled the necklace out of the wreckage. "So sparkly," Harley cooed as she put the necklace around her neck. It was a tight fit since she wore five other necklaces already. Her wrists were lined with gem-studded bracelets, and she wore a diamond ring on every finger.

Harley's eyes went wide when she spotted a diamond-encrusted tiara in the next case. "Ooh! I can be a princess! I can be a princess!" She raised her mallet.

"Here's the key! Here's the key!" the clerk shouted as he darted forward. He quickly unlocked the case, pulled out the headpiece, and handed it to Harley.

Harley gasped as she placed the tiara atop her head. "I feel so . . . elegant." She rounded on the clerk. "Get me a mirror, buster! So I can see how elegant I am!"

"Yes, ma'am," the man said as he gave her a small hand mirror.

"Wowzers," Harley said, gazing at herself.

Her eyes darted past her reflection to see someone in the background. A dark figure stood in the doorway. The masked arrival wore a black cape and had two points atop her head.

Harley spun around. "Batgirl! What a nice surprise!"

The crime fighter darted into the jewelry store. "Caught you red-handed, Harley!" Batgirl's hands moved with lightning speed as she flung three Batarangs.

WHP! WHP! WHP!

Harley barely had time to raise her mallet, blocking the weapons.

THUNK-THUNK! THUNK!

"Wait a minute, Baby Bats," Harley said. "You don't understand."

Batgirl sprinted forward and leaped into the air. "I understand that you're going back to Arkham, where you belong!" She came down with a flying kick.

Harley leaned way back as the Super Hero flew overhead, barely missing her. Batgirl landed and spun around, her cape flowing behind her. She came at the criminal with a series of punches and kicks. Harley held up her mallet to block the attacks.

"If you . . . give me . . . a minute . . . to explain," Harley said between blows.

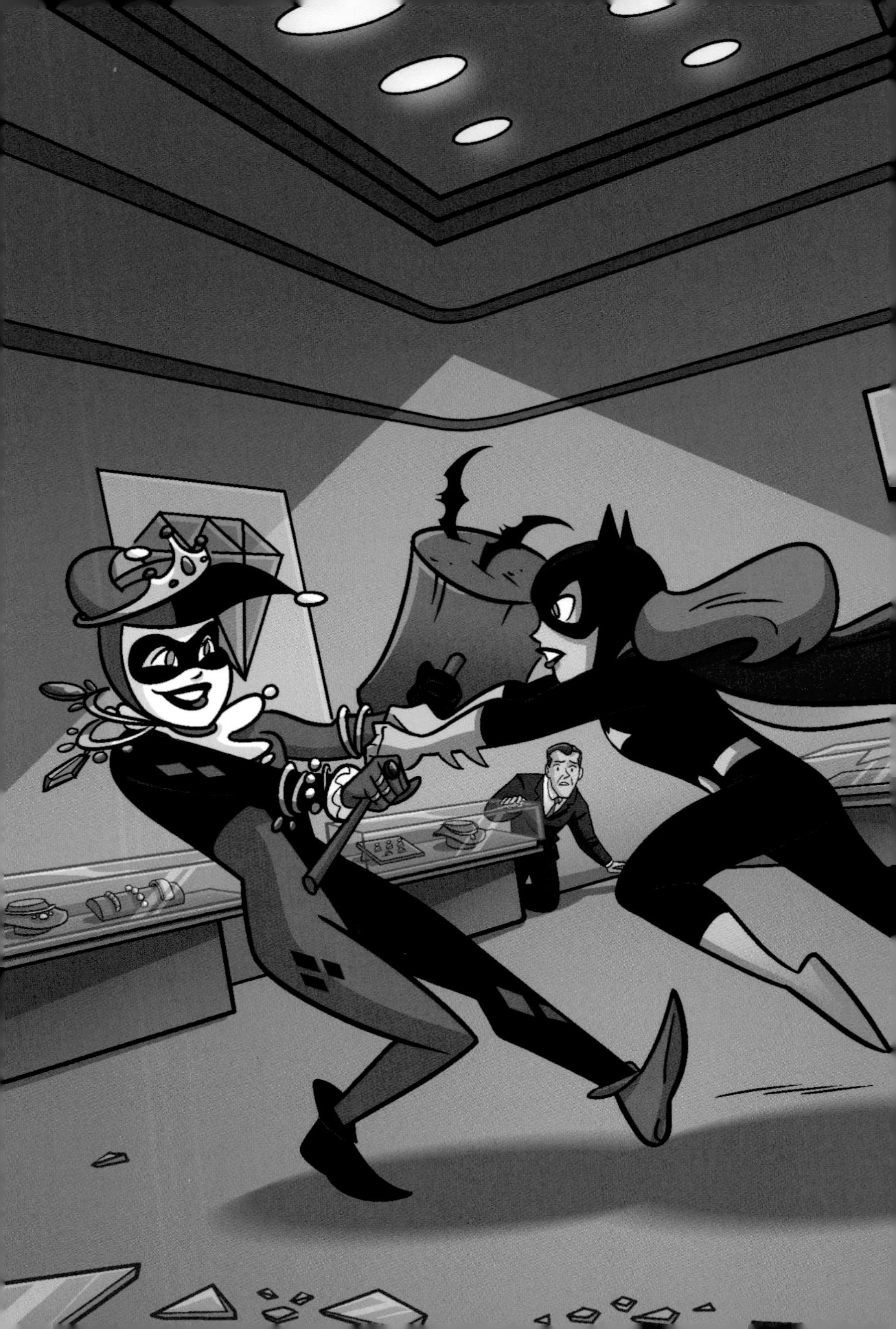

Batgirl didn't let up her attack. She grabbed the mallet's handle and tried to wrestle the weapon away from Harley. Instead, the criminal pulled back, flipping the crime fighter over her head. Batgirl flew across the store and smashed into another display case.

KRASH!

As Batgirl climbed out of the wreckage, Harley raised a hand. "Hang on, Batgirl," she said. "Two things . . ."

Harley spun toward the camera crew. "One . . . tell me you got that shot," she said. "That was way cool!"

One of the two camera operators held up a thumb. Beside him, a woman held a long pole with a microphone on one end. She nodded in approval.

"Two . . . do I look all right?" Harley asked. She reached up and felt her head. "Did I lose my tiara?" Harley giggled. "Whoops. I guess that's three things."

Batgirl brushed bits of glass from her uniform and stepped forward. "What's going on?" she asked as she noticed the group of people recording them with video cameras.

Harley jumped up and down with excitement. Her jewelry rattled with each bounce. "This is my camera crew," she explained. "I'm going to have my very own reality show!"

Batgirl shook her head. "What?"

"It's true," Harley replied. She waved over a bearded man wearing a baseball cap. "This is Stefan. He got me released on good behavior."

"Good behavior?" Batgirl asked. "You?"

"That's right," Stefan said. He ruffled through the papers on his clipboard. He pulled out Harley's release papers and showed them to Batgirl. "It's all legal. We're producing a new reality show and Harley here is going to be the star."

Harley giggled. "Isn't it great?!"

Batgirl nodded at the destruction around them. "And all this . . ."

"Is just for the show," Stefan explained. "Our company will pay for all the damage."

The clerk nodded and grinned. He didn't seem frightened at all anymore.

"It's all an act, Sweetie," Harley explained as she began removing the jewelry. "They wanted to see how I pulled off a robbery. Pretty cool, huh?"

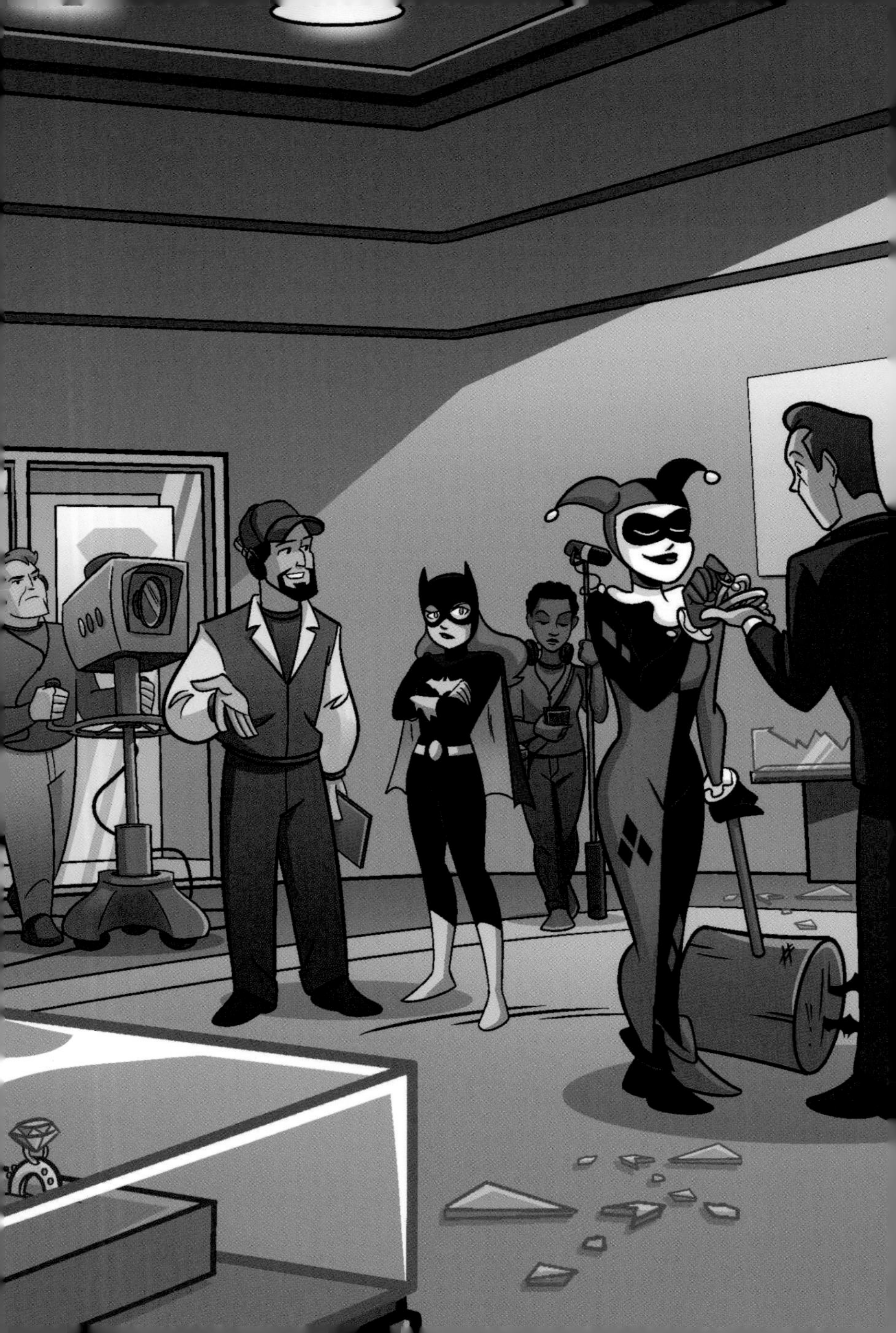

Batgirl crossed her arms. "I thought this was supposed to be a reality show."

Stefan chuckled and gave her a dismissive wave. "Not all reality shows are real." He nodded at Harley. "Sometimes you have to make things happen, to make things more . . . interesting."

"And it was great the way you came in to stop me," Harley added as she excitedly punched the air. "The way you threw those Batarang thingies at me. Real action stuff!"

Stefan ushered one of the camera operators forward. "Can we pick it up after Harley flung you into the display case?" he asked Batgirl.

The crime fighter shook her head. "Oh no. I'm not part of this." She backed toward the door.

"That's all right," Stefan said as Batgirl left the jewelry store. "We can make it look like you threw her off and then got away."

Harley clapped. "You're the best, Stefan!"

Batgirl's eyes narrowed as she stood outside the store. "I know you're up to something, Harley," she said to herself. "And I'm going to find out what it is."

CHAPTER 2

All Fun and Games

The next day, Batgirl was on patrol when she picked up an alert in her earpiece. There was a disturbance at Gotham City Adventure Land. She hit the throttle on her motorcycle and sped toward the scene.

VRRROOOOOM!

As the crime fighter raced into the parking lot, she spotted people racing go-carts on the twisting track. Others played through the mini-golf course as if everything was normal.

But as Batgirl neared the arcade, she saw people streaming out of the exits. Their terrified faces told a different story.

The hero parked her bike and rushed inside. As soon as she was through the door, she spotted what had frightened the guests.

I knew it, Batgirl thought. *After all, who would want to share an arcade with a notorious Super-Villain?*

"What's going on, Harley?" Batgirl asked as she marched past banks of blaring video games and pinging pinball machines. "Are you robbing this place too?"

"You bet your pointy ears I am," Harley replied. "I'm robbing them blind . . . with my amazing Skee-Ball skills!"

Harley rolled a wooden ball up the ramp and it whooshed into the hundred-point hole.

DING-DING-DING-DING-DING!

Bells rang as a line of prize tickets spewed from the machine below. They piled onto the giant mound of tickets at Harley's feet.

Batgirl glanced over and saw that Stefan and his film crew were still recording Harley's every move. The director held up a thumb and grinned.

Harley scooped up her tickets. "Come on, Batgirl," she said. "Let's see what I won!"

The crime fighter shook her head as she followed Harley toward the prize counter. A nervous teenager stood in front of a case full of various toys. Harley dumped the tickets onto the counter. "I'm cashing in!"

As the boy counted her tickets, Harley gazed at the prizes through the glass. "I hope it's a good one."

"That's eight-hundred and fifty-seven tickets," the clerk said as he slid open the case. "So you've won . . . two pencil erasers." He handed them to Harley.

Harley squinted at the tiny prizes. They were shaped like clown heads. Suddenly, her eyes widened and she squealed with delight. "Just what I always wanted!" Harley gave one to Batgirl. "And one for my new bestie!"

"Uh, thanks," Batgirl said as she placed the eraser into a pouch on her Utility Belt. "But this doesn't get you off the hook. I still think you're up to something."

Harley rolled her eyes and draped an arm around Batgirl's shoulders. "Look, if I really wanted to rob this place it would be easy-peasy lemon squeezy!" She pointed to a poster on the wall behind the clerk. "The safe is hidden behind that unicorn poster."

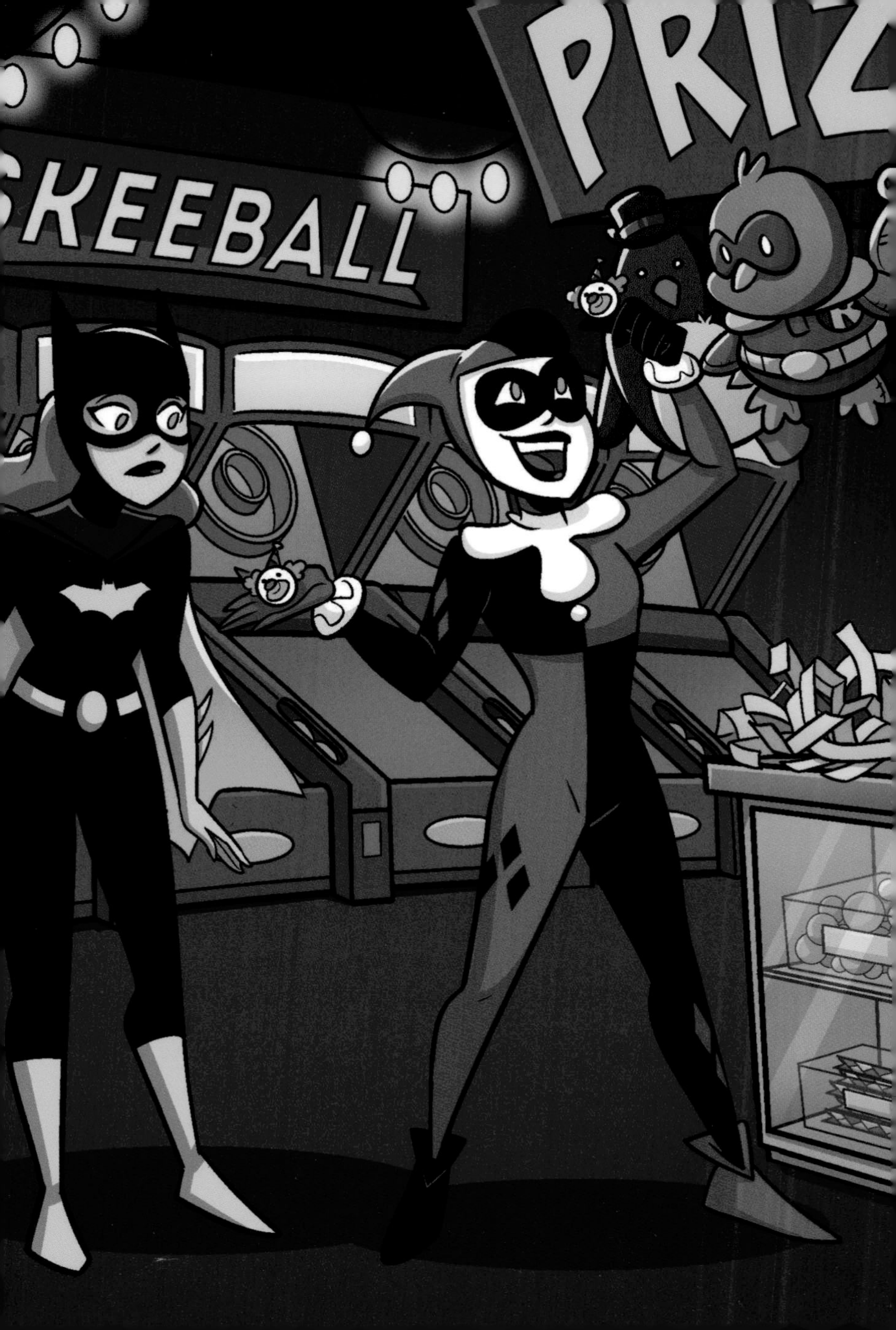
SKEEBALL
PRIZ

The clerk's eyes widened as he glanced over his shoulder. He turned back and gave a weak chuckle.

Harley jutted a thumb at the teen. "And genius here has the combination written on his arm because he keeps forgetting it."

The clerk nervously covered the series of numbers on his forearm.

"It's okay. You can stand down, Batgirl," Harley said. "There's just no crime here." She picked up her mallet and twirled it. "Okay, okay. So maybe they don't like it when you use your own mallet on the whack-a-mole game."

Batgirl glanced over at the wreckage that once was an arcade game. Cartoonish moles were littered among pieces of splintered wood and shards of plastic.

"Which we'll pay for," Stefan added.

Batgirl crossed her arms. "I don't trust you, Harley."

"Trust me? What's not to trust?" Harley asked. "Besides, you can't even catch me!" She gave the crime fighter a playful shove before darting toward the door.

Batgirl caught her footing and took off after the criminal.

"Stay with them!" Stefan ordered as he and the camera crew raced after them.

Outside, people screamed and scattered as Harley bounded across the mini-golf course. She zeroed in on a woman lining up a shot.

"Cinderella story," Harley said as she raised her mallet. "Girl out of nowhere, she lines up the shot . . ." The woman dove for cover as Harley swung at the golf ball.

WHACK!

The ball flew across the course, bounced off a small windmill, and rattled into one of the holes.

"It's in the hole!" Harley cheered.

Batgirl dodged and darted around frightened mini-golfers as she gave chase. The stampede of guests slowed her down, and Harley was already headed toward the go-carts. The criminal somersaulted over the fence and landed inside one of the small vehicles.

SCREEEEE!

Its back tires smoked and squealed as she sped down the track.

Batgirl pulled out her grapnel and fired.

The claw latched onto a tall lamppost and the hero swung above the mini-golf course. Batgirl released the cable when she was above the go-carts. She spread her cape wide, gliding toward the line of empty go-carts. She plopped into the front cart and hit the gas.

SCREEEEEE!

Batgirl gripped the wheel as she raced around the track. Her cape fluttered behind her as she passed other carts, trying to catch up to Harley. She finally spotted the criminal two carts ahead. She passed the one go-cart and moved in on Harley.

Batgirl was about to pull up alongside when two go-carts shot past her. The camera operators drove them, each with one hand on the wheel and the other holding a video camera. One recorded Harley while the other had his camera aimed at Batgirl.

Batgirl's lips tightened as she tried to ignore them. She zipped past the operators and pulled up alongside Harley Quinn.

"Pull over," Batgirl ordered.

"Where's the fun in that?" Harley asked. She jerked the wheel and slammed her go-cart into Batgirl's.

BAM! The crime fighter gripped the steering wheel tighter as she struggled to stay in control.

BAM! Harley slammed against her again.

Batgirl swerved across the track, barely missing one of the camera operators. She jerked the wheel and came back alongside Harley. The criminal shouted something, but Batgirl couldn't make it out over the roar of the engines.

"What?" Batgirl asked.

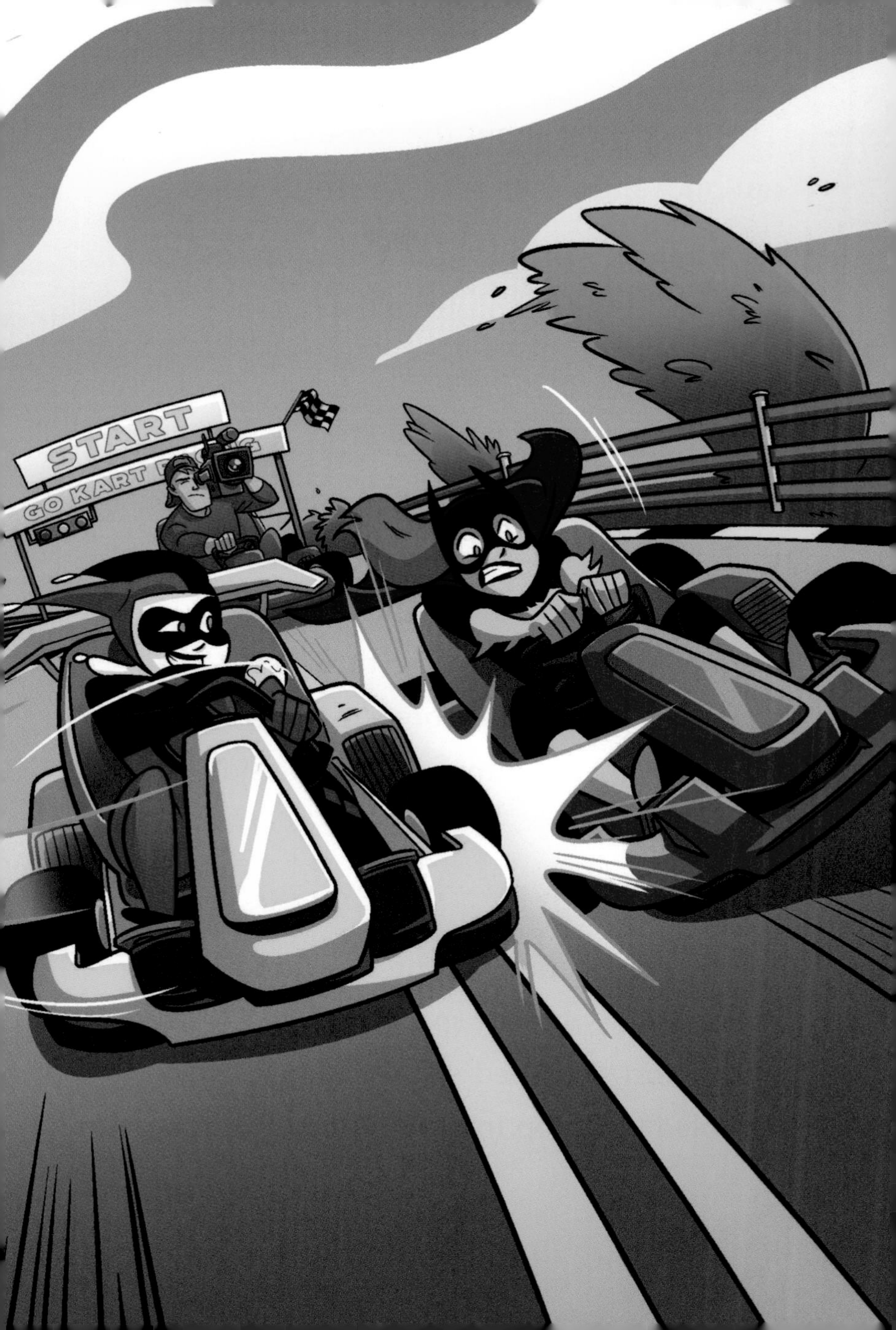
START
GO KART

Harley replied but the noise drowned her out once more.

Batgirl hit the gas and pulled up next to Harley. "What?" Batgirl asked again.

Harley pointed forward. "I said watch out for this next turn. It's a doozy!"

Batgirl's head snapped forward just in time to see the tight bend in the track ahead. Harley and the camera operators slowed as they zipped around the turn. But Batgirl was going too fast. Before she could hit the brakes, her cart slammed into the side of the track.

WHAP!

Her go-cart flew off the track and rolled through the air. Dirt sprayed ahead of her as her cart slammed into the ground and tumbled to a stop in the middle of the course.

Batgirl moaned and shook her head. Her go-cart had ended up on its side. As the motor finally silenced, she unbuckled her seat belt and tumbled from the smashed vehicle. She slowly got to her feet and glanced around the adventure park.

Harley and the camera crew were nowhere to be found.

CHAPTER 3

Big Chase Scene

"Oh my!" a woman said as she scooped up her two children and ran out of the park.

A young couple left their picnic and ran in terror toward the nearby parking lot. A cyclist nearly wiped out as he ran his bicycle off the sidewalk.

Harley glanced around at the fleeing people. "What's the matter?" she asked. "Haven't you ever seen someone going for a walk with her babies before?"

She shrugged as she continued her stroll down the sidewalk. Her large hyenas, Crackers and Giggles, pulled at their leashes as the three of them ambled through the park. The two beasts cackled with laughter as they bared their sharp teeth at the frightened people.

Harley sighed with delight as she casually walked her pets through the park. She wore a large hat and a pair of sunglasses. Stefan and the camera crew kept pace with her. One camera operator recorded Harley while the other trained his camera on the escaping public.

As Harley neared an oak tree, she spotted a familiar face. Batgirl leaned against her motorcycle in the shade. Harley squealed and waved at the crime fighter.

"What are you up to now?" Batgirl asked.

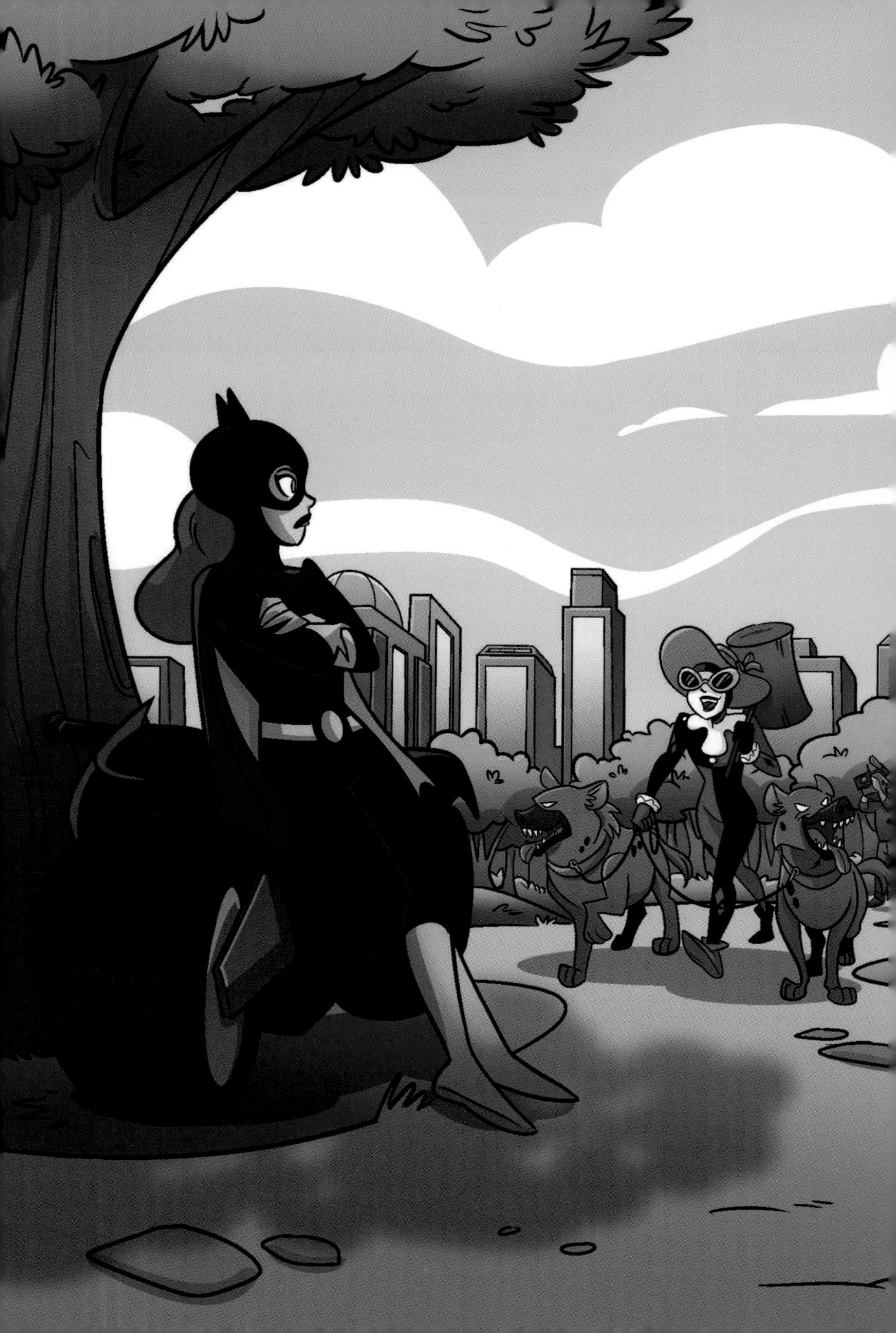

Harley shrugged. "Oh, you know. Just getting some more footage of a typical day in the life of Harley Quinn. Pretty cool, huh?"

"A typical day?" Batgirl asked. "Taking two hyenas for a stroll through the park?"

Harley rolled her eyes. "Don't worry. It's all legal-like," she replied. "Show her what I'm talking about, Stefan."

The director shuffled through the papers on his clipboard and pulled out a form. "We have permission from the zoo to take her, uh . . . babies out for the day."

Batgirl examined the piece of paper. Sure enough, everything was just as they had said.

"You may have these guys fooled," Batgirl said. "But not me. I know you're up to something."

"You're right. I'm up to nine thousand steps," Harley replied. "Now, if you'll excuse me, I have to get the rest of my steps in for the day. A girl's got to stay in shape."

Harley was about to continue her stroll when Batgirl's hand touched the side of her mask. Harley stopped in her tracks.

"Ooh! I know what that means," the criminal said. "That's what Bats does when he hears about a crime happening." She jumped up and down excitedly. "Tell me I'm right! I'm right, aren't I?"

Batgirl sighed. "You're right, Harley. Someone just hijacked an armored truck full of money." She climbed onto her bike.

"Yes! I knew it!" Harley turned to Stefan. "How about some footage of me and Batgirl here catching some crooks?"

"Absolutely!" Stefan replied.

"Absolutely not!" Batgirl said as she started her motorcycle.

Harley shoved the leashes into Stefan's hands and threw off her hat and sunglasses. She twirled her mallet and hopped onto the back of Batgirl's bike as she sped away.

"What are you doing?" Batgirl asked as she pulled out of the park.

"Only being part of the best team-up ever," Harley replied. "Me and my bat-bestie fightin' crime in Gotham City!"

Batgirl zigzagged through heavy traffic as she drove her bike through the streets. "Get off, Harley," Batgirl ordered. "Now!"

"That wouldn't be too safe now, would it?" Harley asked with a grin. "And if you stop, the bad guys might get away, huh?"

Batgirl shook her head and hit the throttle. The motorcycle bucked forward as she poured on the speed. She zipped around corners and raced through narrow alleyways. After another turn, the armored truck was ahead of them. Batgirl leaned forward as they slowly caught up to the stolen vehicle.

VROOOM-VROOOOOOM!

Two other motorcycles raced up alongside them. Batgirl tensed, preparing to fight off an attack. Were they with the crooks who stole the truck? She glanced over and spotted them aiming something at her. She was relieved when she realized the riders were only holding cameras.

"Hey, gang!" Harley waved at the mobile camera crew. "We can call it the *HARLEY AND BATGIRL SHOW*, if you want," she told the crime fighter. "I get top billing, of course."

Batgirl ignored Harley and the trailing motorcycles as she concentrated on the road. She slowly closed the gap between her and the armored truck. She leaned to the left, preparing to go around the large vehicle. The truck swerved to the left, blocking her path. She tried to pass on the right, but the same thing happened. Batgirl reached for her Utility Belt and pulled out her grapnel. She aimed it at the back of the truck.

Just then, Harley hopped up onto the seat and rode it like a surfboard.

"What are you doing?" Batgirl asked as she tried to keep the bike steady.

"I got this," Harley replied. "Hit the brakes!"

"What?" Batgirl asked.

"I said BRAKE!" Harley shouted. "Now!"

SKREECH!

Batgirl hit the brakes and her back tire came off the ground. Harley flew off the back of the bike and soared toward the armored truck. With her mallet in one hand, she latched onto the roof of the truck with the other. She dangled for a moment, swinging back and forth, as the speeding vehicle swerved through traffic.

Harley grunted as she swung herself onto the top of the truck. Then she giggled as she skipped across the roof. When she reached the front, she flipped over the edge and landed on the hood. The crooks stared at her in disbelief through the windshield.

"This is way better than whack-a-mole!" Harley said as she raised her mallet.

SMASH!

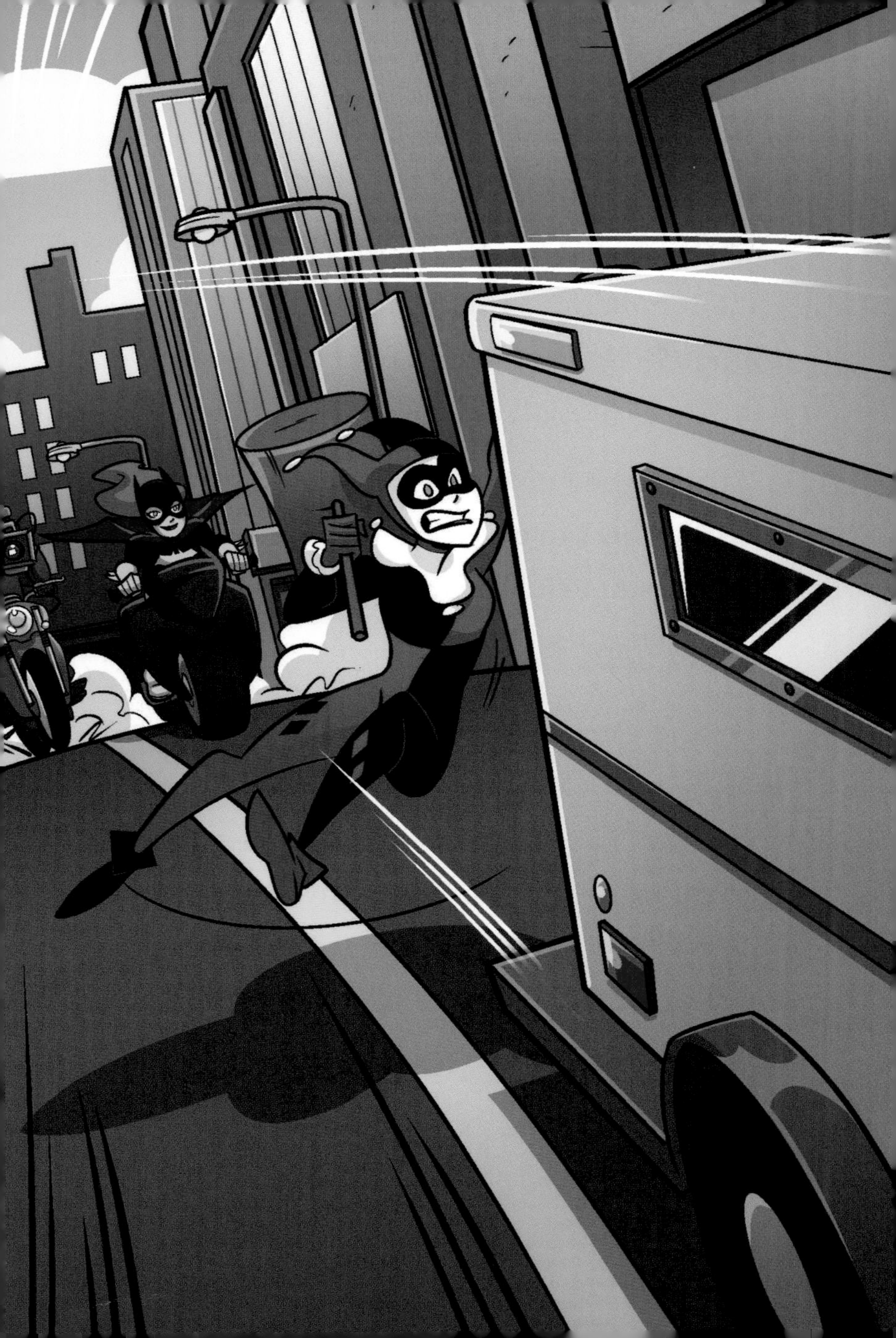

The glass shattered as her mallet came down on the windshield. The truck jerked beneath her feet, but she stayed on the hood.

"I'm making a citizen's arrest," Harley announced with a laugh. "I know. Crazy, right?"

She reached down and yanked the steering wheel to one side. The truck veered to the left and slammed into a fire hydrant.

BAM! WHOOSH!

As the truck came to a stop, Harley flipped off the hood. She landed on the sidewalk as water from the broken hydrant rained down from above. The Mistress of Mayhem spread her arms wide and spun around. "They didn't say it was going to rain today!"

SCREEEE! SCREE-SCREEEEE!

Batgirl and the camera crew screeched to a stop beside the wrecked truck. The crime fighter was off her bike and cuffing the criminals as soon as they stumbled out of the cab.

"I told you we'd make a great team!" Harley said as she climbed onto the back of one of the camera bikes. "Let me know if you need help catching any more bad guys." She gave a wave as they sped off down the street.

Batgirl shook her head as she watched them leave.

CHAPTER 4

A Smash Hit

The next day, Batgirl took a different approach with the Harley Quinn problem. She did a little detective work, retracing the criminal's steps over the past few days. The first stop was the jewelry store where she had initially come across Harley and her new reality show camera crew.

"I was robbed," the clerk told her. "After that strange lady left, a bunch of masked crooks came in and took everything."

Batgirl heard a similar story when she returned to Gotham City Adventure Land.

"They knew right where the safe was hidden," the young clerk said. He held up his arm. "And they knew where to find the combination."

Batgirl knew there was nothing to steal at the park. But when she followed up on the armored truck heist, she made a disturbing discovery.

"We picked up the crooks you left for us," a police officer told her. "But there was no money in the truck by the time we got there."

Batgirl was furious. She knew Harley Quinn had been up to no good, and she should have taken her in when she had the chance. Worse than that, she had led Harley right to the armored truck full of cash.

For the rest of the day, Batgirl searched the city for Harley and her camera crew. She tried every place that might attract the Clown Princess of Crime—a joke shop, a carnival, a Hula-Hoop factory. Nothing. She even swung by the zoo, but Crackers and Giggles were safely back in their enclosure.

By late afternoon, she finally got a lead when someone matching Harley's description was spotted smashing things at the Gotham City Coliseum. Batgirl hit the gas as she sped over to the latest crime scene. Once she went inside, however, the crime fighter realized just how exact the tip had been.

SMASH! KRASH! BAM! SMASH!

The coliseum floor was covered in dirt as a demolition derby was in full swing. Several dented cars roared around the arena as they purposely tried to crash into each other.

One car in particular was doing most of the smashing. A red and black car dodged two attacking vehicles before it rammed into the back of a third.

KRASH!

"Woo-hoo!" the driver cheered in an all-too-familiar voice.

Batgirl whipped out her grapnel and aimed it toward a beam above the arena.

POP! WRRRRRR! Once the grapnel clamped tight, Batgirl swung out over the roaring cars. She released the cable and somersaulted in midair. She landed on the hood of Harley Quinn's car.

Harley's eyes lit up with joy. "Hiya, Bat-Bestie! It's about time you got here!"

"You're not getting away this time," Batgirl said.

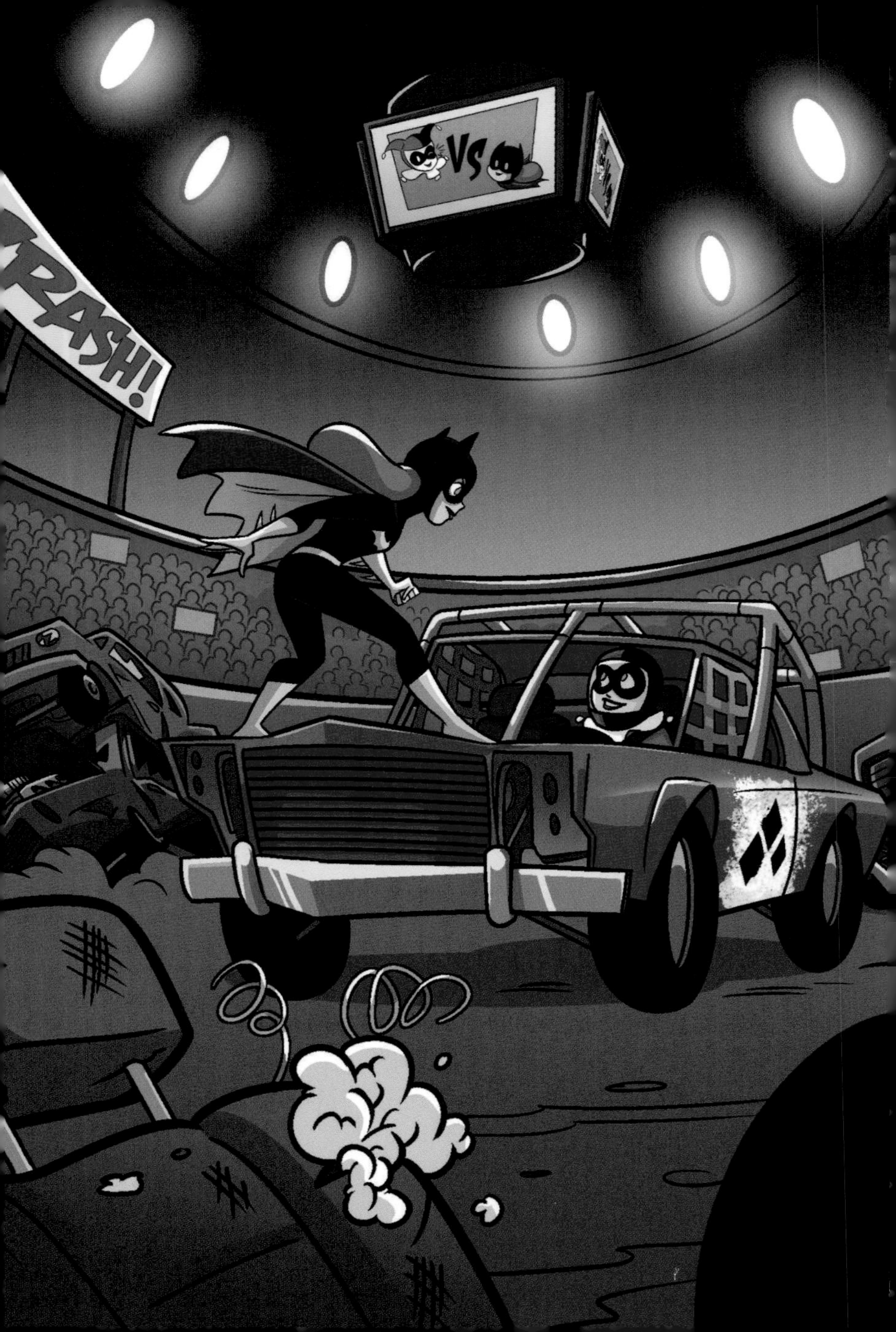
RASH!
VS

"Getting away with what?" Harley asked. "I signed up for this, paid my admission fee. And as you can see, I'm totally dominating these other bums!"

KRASH! Batgirl barely stayed on her feet as Harley crashed into another car.

"I'm talking about the robberies," Batgirl explained. "The jewelry store? The arcade? The armored truck?"

"Nope." Harley shook her head. "Doesn't ring a bell. I think I would know if I had robbed those places."

"Let's go, Harley," Batgirl said. "You're coming with me."

Harley shook her head. "Geeesh! Enough with the shop talk." She hit the gas. "Besides, Stefan and the gang cooked up something special just for you."

BAM! Harley crashed into a car parked off to the side. Batgirl was flung off her feet before tumbling across the hood of the other car. She flew through the open windshield and landed in the empty driver's seat. The car was painted black and yellow, with a large yellow Bat-Symbol on the hood. A matching helmet sat in the passenger seat.

Harley backed her car away and revved her engine.

VROOOM-VROOOM!

"That's how you want to play, huh?" Batgirl asked as she threw on the helmet and strapped herself in.

Plumes of dirt erupted from the back of Harley's car as it lurched forward. Batgirl barely got her own car started and moving before Harley closed in.

SMASH!

Harley clipped the back of Batgirl's car, spinning her around. The audience cheered. Batgirl hit the gas and got clear before Harley could move in for another hit.

"Let's give you a taste of your own medicine," Batgirl said as she spun the steering wheel. Her car drifted into a turn as she pulled away from Harley. She whirled back around and aimed for the front of Harley's car.

BAM!

Harley bounced in her seat. "Good one!" she shouted.

Batgirl didn't let up. She hit the gas, dodged two more cars, and came back again toward Harley. She rammed the back of the red and black car.

WHAM!

Batgirl grinned. "Okay, this is way better than go-carts."

She floored the gas pedal, pushing Harley's car around the arena. Two more derby cars closed in from either side. Batgirl hit the brakes, and Harley's car kept going. The other cars zipped in on either side, smashing Harley's car between them.

WHA-POW!

Smoke poured out from under Harley's hood as her engine died. She turned the ignition but it wouldn't restart.

"That's okay," Harley said as she climbed out of the window. "I have a backup!" She ran across the field.

"Watch out, Harley!" Batgirl shouted as the criminal dodged cars along the way.

Harley disappeared into a large, dark corridor. Batgirl tried to follow, but she was too busy dodging other derby drivers.

When the hero finally made her way to the opening, she was suddenly blinded by two giant headlights. Batgirl hit the brakes as the ground beneath her vibrated.

VROOOOOOOOM!

"Aw-yeah! Mama likes!" Harley yelled as she drove a giant monster truck into the arena. The enormous tires kicked up dirt and plumes of fire erupted from twin exhaust pipes behind the cab. The truck's huge engine revved and the audience roared with delight.

Batgirl hit the gas and spun the wheel. Dirt sprayed across the field as she made a sharp turn, trying to get away from the gigantic vehicle.

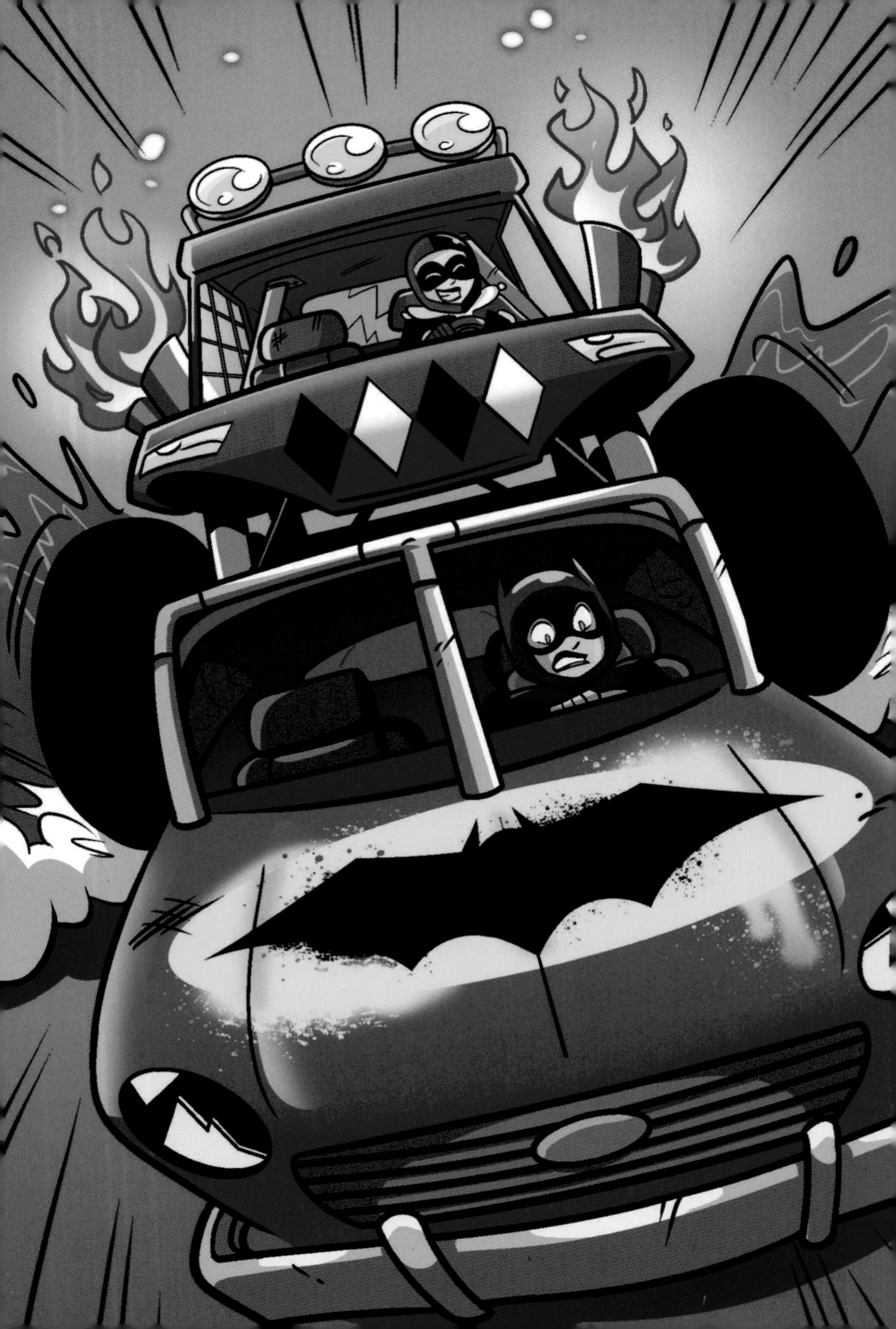

Harley giggled as she rumbled after her. Other drivers leaped out of their windows before the monster truck rolled over their cars. **KRACK! KRUNCH! KRASH!** It smashed them as if they were toys.

Batgirl pushed the gas pedal all the way down, but Harley still gained on her. "Enough of this," she said as she pulled out a Batarang. She used the sharp weapon to pin the gas pedal to the floor. Then she climbed through the open windshield and fired her grapnel.

POP!

It latched onto the ceiling and pulled her clear. The monster truck hit Batgirl's car like a ramp. "Wheeee!" Harley cried as her truck launched into the air. It flew over a white van parked in an access corridor and smashed through a wall.

KA-SMASH!

Dirt and pieces of brick flew everywhere.

When the dust settled, Batgirl swung down and landed on the hood of the monster truck. She whipped off her helmet and pulled a pair of handcuffs from her Utility Belt.

"Hey!" Harley said, looking past the crime fighter. "What are you guys doing in there? You missed my big finish!"

Batgirl spun around and her eyes widened when she gazed through the hole in the wall. The arena vault was on the other side. Two security guards were tied up, while Stefan and his crew robbed the large safe.

"I knew it!" Batgirl shouted.

CHAPTER 5

Chase Scene, Take Two

CLIK-CLIK!

Batgirl reached into the monster truck's cab and snapped the handcuffs onto Harley's wrists.

"What are these for?" Harley asked. "I didn't do anything!"

Batgirl pointed toward the vault. "Hello?! Your gang is robbing the place!"

Harley pulled off her helmet and shook her head. "They're not my gang. They're my camera crew." Harley leaned over to get a better look at the crew. "Who were supposed to record all my smashing glory!"

Stefan and the others didn't reply. They hustled bags of money through a nearby doorway and into the parked van.

"What about the jewelry store?" Batgirl asked her. "Or the arcade? The missing money from the armored truck?"

"I didn't steal anything from those places," Harley explained. "All that was for the show. I told you that."

"They were all robbed, Harley. You and your crew went back and robbed them after I left." Batgirl said. "That reality show story of yours was just a cover."

"Nuh-uh!" Harley said, shaking her head. "Stefan said I'm going to be a star!"

Batgirl pointed to the crew piling into the van. "Then why aren't they filming you?" she asked.

Harley looked from Batgirl to the crew. Then she looked from the crew to Batgirl. And then from Batgirl back to the crew again. Her mouth dropped open.

"Those low-down, dirty rats!" Harley shouted. "They used me to find all the best places to rob!"

Batgirl chuckled and crossed her arms. "Yeah, right."

"It's true," Harley pleaded. She pointed to the van as it drove down the large corridor toward the exit. "And now they're getting away!"

Harley put the truck in gear and backed out of the hole. Batgirl—still perched on the hood—barely stayed on her feet as the monster truck pulled into the corridor and raced after the van.

Batgirl quickly scrambled into the cab and strapped herself into the passenger seat. She bounced up and down as Harley's monster truck followed the van out of the stadium.

"Here," Harley said as she handed over the handcuffs. "Save these for those rat finks in the van."

Batgirl took the cuffs, amazed at how quickly Harley had escaped them. She gazed at the grim look of determination on Harley's face as she drove.

"You really had no idea they were robbing those places, did you?" the hero asked.

"That's what I said," Harley replied. "And now I have a score to settle."

The van zipped around traffic ahead of them. Cars and trucks quickly pulled over as Harley's monster truck rumbled after it.

"Best team-up ever!" Harley shouted as she floored the gas pedal. The truck rocketed toward the van.

SCREEEEE!

The van's tires squealed as it took a hard left onto a narrow street.

WOMP-WOMP-WOMP-WOMP!

The monster truck's giant tires bounced and skidded as it barely made the turn behind them. Unfortunately, the street was too narrow for the monster truck.

KRASH! KRUNCH! KRINKLE! KRASH!

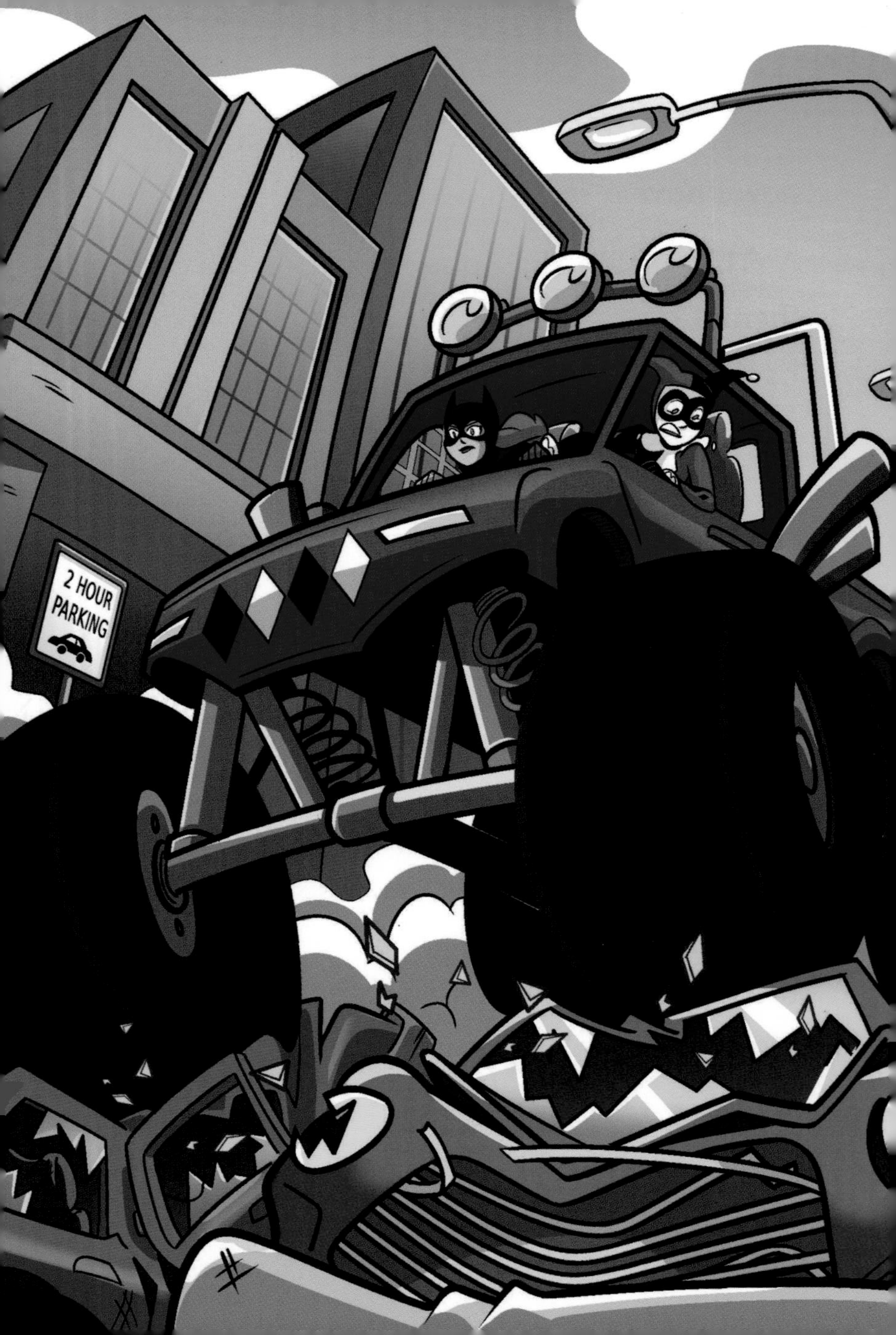
2 HOUR
PARKING

The tires rumbled over empty parked cars on either side of the street.

"Whoops!" Harley shouted as she bobbed up and down. "Sorry about that! That'll probably buff right out!"

The van began to pull away.

"This isn't working, Harley," Batgirl said. She pressed a button on her Utility Belt.

"Worse than that, we're almost out of gas," Harley added. "These things don't get the best gas mileage, you know."

As the truck slowed, Batgirl's motorcycle pulled to a stop beside them. The crime fighter leaped out of the window and onto the seat. Harley snatched up her mallet and was right behind her.

"Hey!" Harley shouted. "You're not going without me!"

"Well, come on then," Batgirl said as she revved the engine.

Once Harley hit the seat, Batgirl hit the throttle. The motorcycle pulled a wheelie as it sped down the street.

After a few twists and turns, the white van came into view once more. Batgirl swerved through traffic as she slowly caught up to the fleeing criminals.

As they closed the gap, Harley stood on the seat and readied her mallet. "All right, Bat-Bestie," she said. "You know what to do."

Batgirl poured on the speed and the motorcycle sped up to the back of the van. Then, at the last minute, she hit the brakes. Her back wheel flew off the street and Harley flew off the seat. She flipped in midair and landed on the van's roof.

Batgirl swerved right and pulled alongside the speeding vehicle. Meanwhile, Harley ran across the top, before sliding down to the hood. Stefan and the crew looked terrified as they stared up at her through the windshield.

"All right, gang," she said. "You know how this ends. Want to stop the easy way or the hard way?" She raised her mallet above her head. "Batter up!"

SCREEEEECH! The van skidded to a stop. Harley flipped off the hood and lightly touched down on the street.

"Aw, stinkeroony!" she exclaimed. "The easy way isn't as fun."

Batgirl pulled to a stop as the criminals poured out of the van. They each had their hands up, ready to surrender. In no time at all, Batgirl had each of them cuffed.

"I told you we made a great team," Harley said with a grin.

"Maybe so." Batgirl nodded. "Have you thought of crime fighting instead of being a criminal?"

"I don't know," Harley replied with a shrug. She held a finger on either side of her head. "I can't see myself with pointed ears."

Harley turned around, threw her mallet over her shoulder, and skipped down the sidewalk. "See you around, Bat-Bestie."

As the Clown Princess of Crime left, Batgirl reached into her Utility Belt. She pulled out the pencil eraser and balanced it in the palm of her hand.

"See you around, Harley Quinn," the hero replied with a smile.

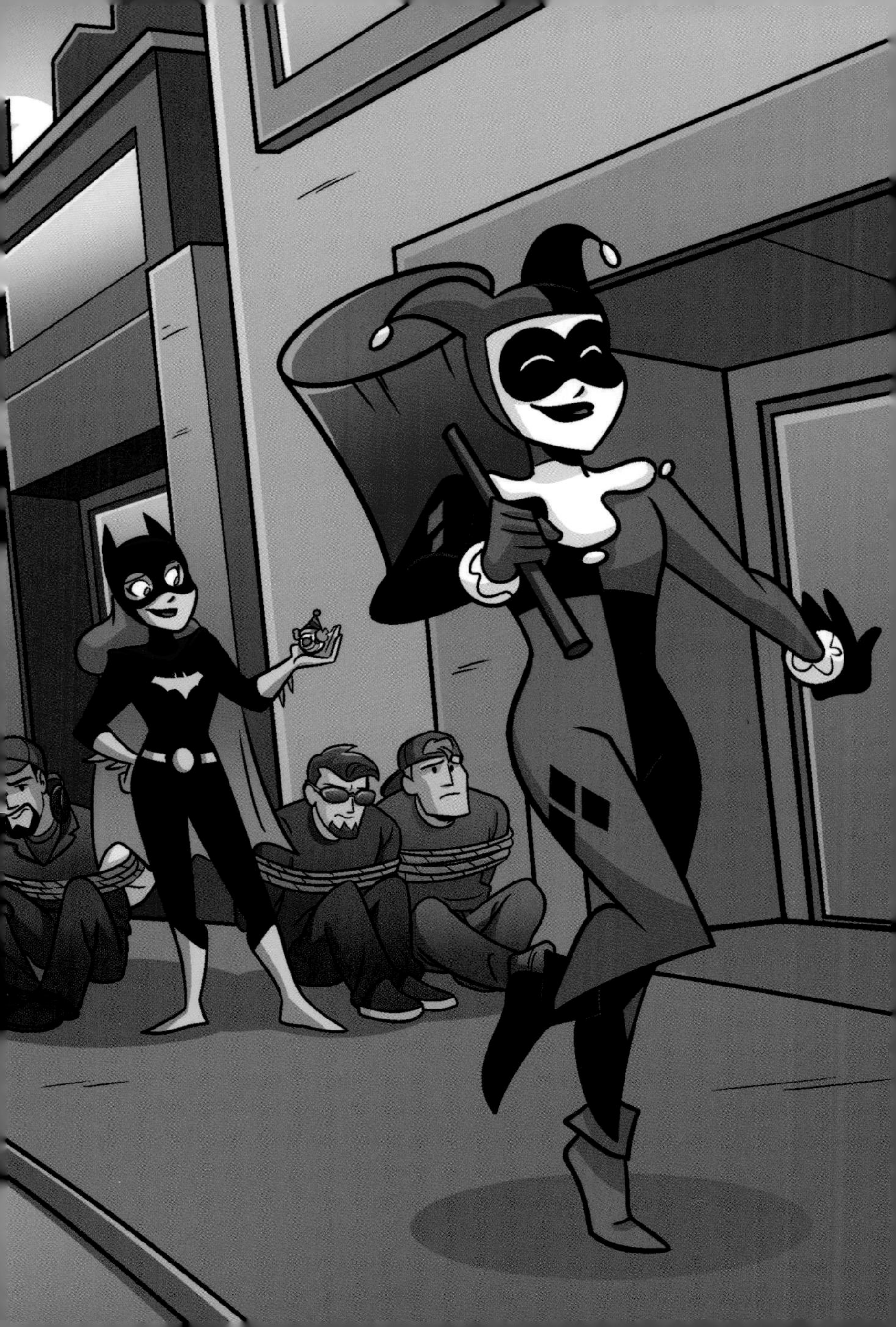

BATGIRL

REAL NAME: Barbara Gordon
OCCUPATION: Crime Fighter
BASE: Gotham City

BIOGRAPHY: Growing up in Gotham City, Barbara Gordon often saw Batman bring justice to those who needed it most. But when her father, Police Commissioner James Gordon, was arrested for a crime he didn't commit, she couldn't sit back and hope for a hero. Donning a Batsuit of her own design, she set out to clear her father's name without his knowledge. With her brilliant mind and a mastery of martial arts, Barbara did more than simply free her father. She became Batgirl and earned a permanent place in the Batman family.

HARLEY'S FRIENDS AND FOES

FRIENDS

Harley & Poison Ivy

Harley & The Joker

Catwoman

Giggles, Harley, & Crackers

FOES

Batman

Robin

Batgirl

Batwoman

Batwing

photo by M. A. Steele

MICHAEL ANTHONY STEELE has been in the entertainment industry for more than 27 years, writing for television, movies, and video games. He has authored more than 120 books for exciting characters and brands including Batman, Superman, Wonder Woman, Spider-Man, Shrek, Scooby-Doo, LEGO City, Garfield, Winx Club, Night at the Museum, and The Penguins of Madagascar. Steele lives on a ranch in Texas, but he enjoys meeting his readers when he visits schools and libraries all across the country. For more information, visit MichaelAnthonySteele.com.

illustration by Sarah Leuver

SARAH LEUVER is a San Francisco Bay Area-based comic artist who has worked on series such as Teen Titans Go! and DC Superhero Girls. When she's not drawing super heroes for work, she can usually be found drawing them for fun. In the rare instances where she isn't drawing, she enjoys spending time with her family and her dog, Oliver.

GLOSSARY

arcade (ar-KADE)—a covered area with machines for amusement, such as pinball and video games

dominate (DAH-muh-nayt)—to control because of strength and power

footage (FUT-age)—material recorded on video

gas mileage (GASS MILE-age)—the number of miles a vehicle can travel using a gallon of fuel

grapnel (GRAP-nuhl)—a grappling hook connected to a rope that can be fired like a gun

heist (HYEST)—an armed robbery

hijack (HYE-jak)—to take illegal control of a vehicle

hyena (hi-EE-na)—a wild animal that looks somewhat like a dog

ignition (ig-NISH-uhn)—the electrical system of a vehicle that uses power from the battery to start the engine

mallet (MAL-it)—a hammer with a short handle and a heavy wooden head

throttle (THROT-uhl)—a lever, pedal, or handle used to control the speed of an engine

tiara (tee-AR-uh)—a piece of jewelry that looks like a crown

TALK ABOUT IT

1. Why do you think Harley decided to be on a reality TV show? If you had the chance, would you want to be part of a reality TV show too? Explain your answer.

2. Harley and Batgirl team up in this story, even though they are usually enemies. What makes them a good team? Do you think they should team up more often?

3. Batgirl doesn't believe Harley when she claims she didn't know her film crew was committing crimes behind her back. Would you have believed her? Why or why not?

1. Harley and Batgirl have very different personalities. Which character do you like best? Write a short paragraph explaining why you prefer one character over the other.

2. Harley's monster truck is painted in colors that match her costume. If Batgirl had her own monster truck, what would it look like? Write a short paragraph describing a Batgirl monster truck and draw a picture of it.

3. At the end of the story, Harley skips away down the sidewalk. Where do you think she goes? Write a new chapter about what Harley does next in Gotham City.

READ THEM ALL!

The Harley and Batgirl Show

by Michael Anthony Steele · illustrated by Sarah Leuver

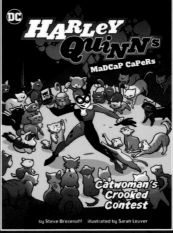

Catwoman's Crooked Contest

by Steve Brezenoff · illustrated by Sarah Leuver

Poison Ivy's Big Boss in Bloom

by Michael Anthony Steele · illustrated by Sara Foresti

The Joker Hideout Heist

by Steve Brezenoff · illustrated by Sara Foresti